I Like Dogs

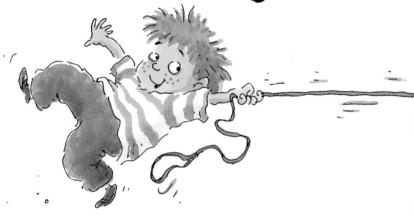

Barbara   Mitchelhill
Illustrated   by   René   Williams

Rigby

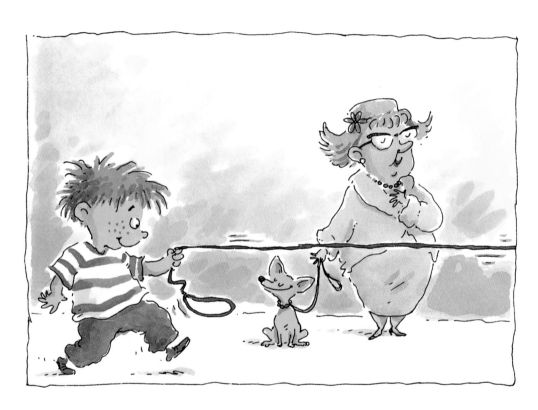

I like the little dog.

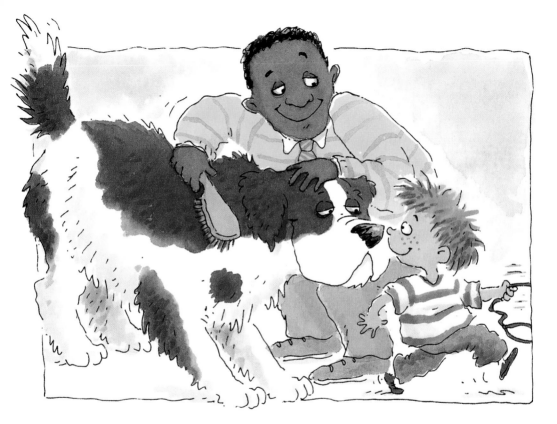

I like the big dog.

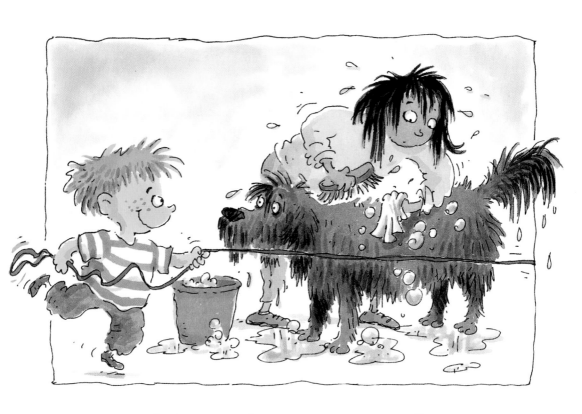

I like the wet dog.

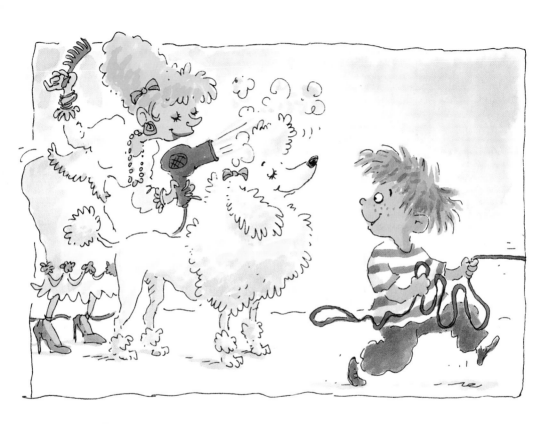

I like the dry dog.

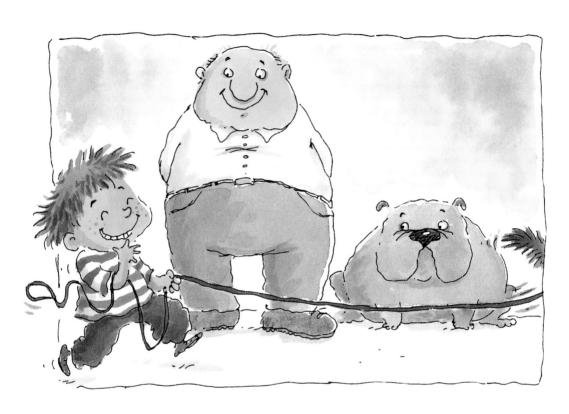

I like the fat dog.

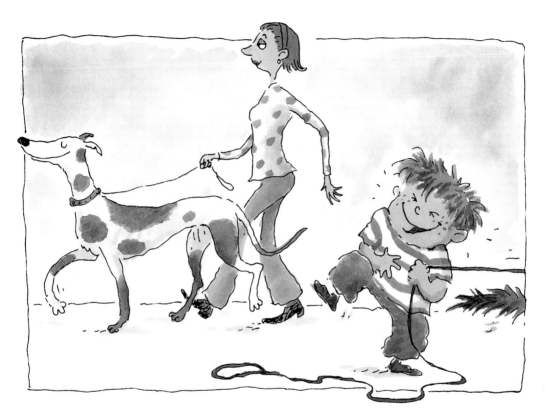

I like the thin dog . . .

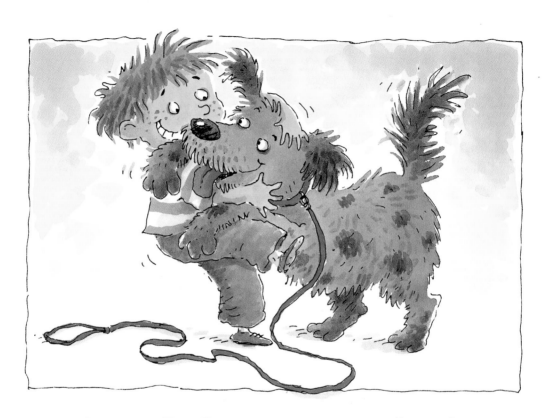

but I **love** my dog!